Budgie & Boo

David McPhail

Abrams Books for Young Readers, New York

The illustrations in this book were made with
pen and ink and watercolor on paper.

McPhail, David, 1940–
Budgie and Boo / written and illustrated by David McPhail.
p. cm.
Summary: Budgie grows flowers and Boo grows vegetables,
and they are the best of friends.
ISBN 978-0-8109-8324-3
[1. Best friends—Fiction. 2. Friendship—Fiction.
3. Rabbits—Fiction. 4. Bears—Fiction.] I. Title.

PZ7.M2427Dax 2009
[E]—dc22
2008008225

Book design by Chad W. Beckerman

Printed and bound in China
10 9 8 7 6 5 4 3 2 1

Abrams Books for Young Readers are available at special discounts when
purchased in quantity for premiums and promotions as well as fundraising
or educational use. Special editions can also be created to specification. For
details, contact specialmarkets@hnabooks.com or the address below.

HNA ▪▪▪▪▪
harry n. abrams, inc.
a subsidiary of La Martinière Groupe
115 West 18th Street
New York, NY 10011
www.hnabooks.com

For John O'Connor, who gave me the name . . .
and for Chad and Tamar,
who make my life difficult,
but to a good end.

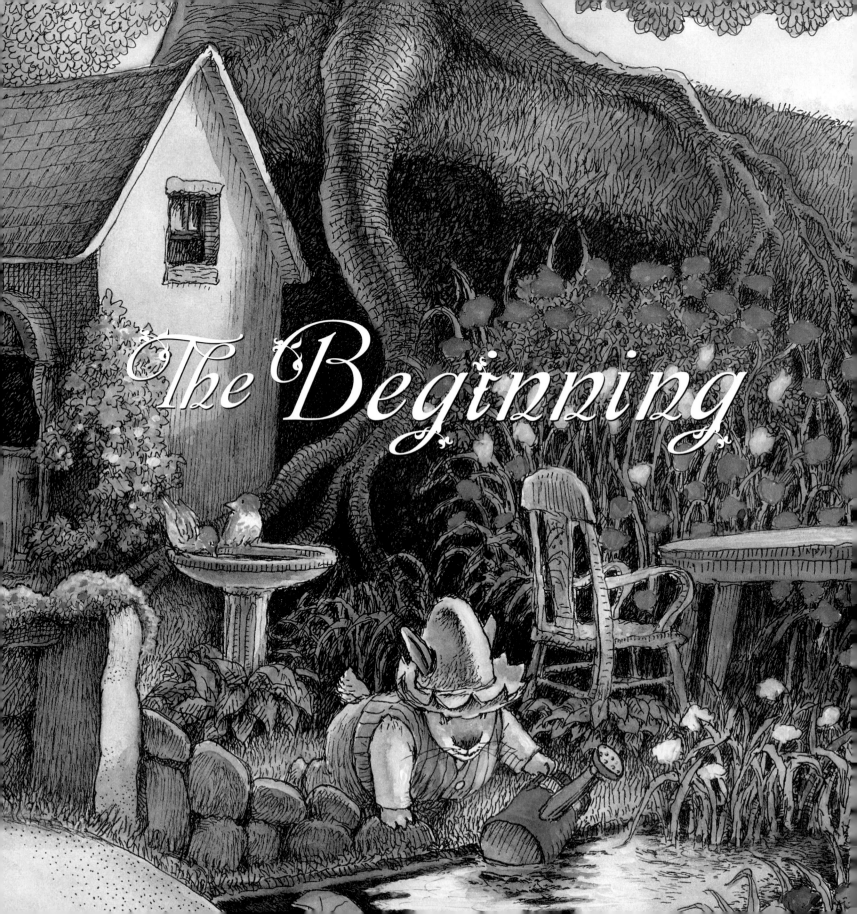

The Beginning

Budgie was a bear. Boo was a bunny. Budgie grew flowers. Boo grew vegetables. Boo's vegetables were the tastiest, and nobody grew flowers as beautiful as Budgie's.

Budgie and Boo woke up as soon as the birds began to sing. By sunrise, they both were hard at work in the garden. Budgie chopped weeds, and Boo carried water from the well.

Budgie and Boo were the best gardeners, who
decided to be the best of friends.
And they were.

Budgie slept quietly. Boo always snored.
One morning, Boo woke up suddenly.

"Are you awake, Budgie?" he whispered loudly.

"I am now, Boo," Budgie groaned. "What's the matter?"

"My nose is wet!" Boo answered.

"Maybe you're not feeling well," said Budgie.

"I feel fine," said Boo. "Except that my nose is wet."

Budgie turned his flashlight on and looked up. A big drop of water was forming on the ceiling. It fell onto Boo's nose.

"It's raining inside our house!" cried Boo.
"It's not raining inside our house," Budgie said.
"There's a leak in the roof."

"Oh, dear," said Boo.
"Don't worry," said Budgie, as he pushed Boo's bed
against the wall. "Now the water won't drip on your nose."

"That's why you are my best friend," Boo said.
"Why?" asked Budgie.
"Because you always know how to fix things," said Boo.
"Now it's time to fix breakfast," Budgie said.
And they did.

Afternoon

Budgie looked out at the garden. Boo waited
for the rain to stop. Finally it did.

"Now it's my turn to fix something," Boo said.

Boo got the ladder from the toolshed and leaned
it against the side of the house. Then he started up.
"I'll find the leak in the roof," he called over his
shoulder. "You bring up the tools."

Budgie went into the toolshed and put some tools in his wheelbarrow. Then he pushed the wheelbarrow to the ladder.

"I found the leak!" Boo said. "One of the shingles on our roof lifted, and the rain came in."

Budgie carefully climbed up the ladder.
"Here is a tool," Budgie said.
"I don't need a rake," Boo said.

Budgie went back down the ladder and returned with another tool.

"Here is a tool," Budgie said.
"I don't need a shovel," said Boo.

Budgie took the shovel down and returned with another tool.

"Here is a tool," Budgie said.
"I don't need a hoe," Boo said. "This is a *roof*,
not a *garden*! What I need is a hammer and some nails."

Budgie climbed down the ladder once more
and returned with a hammer and some nails.

"Now I can fix the leak in the roof," Boo said.
"I will stick to gardening," Budgie said.
And they laughed.

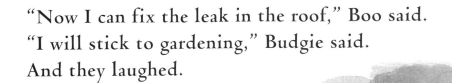

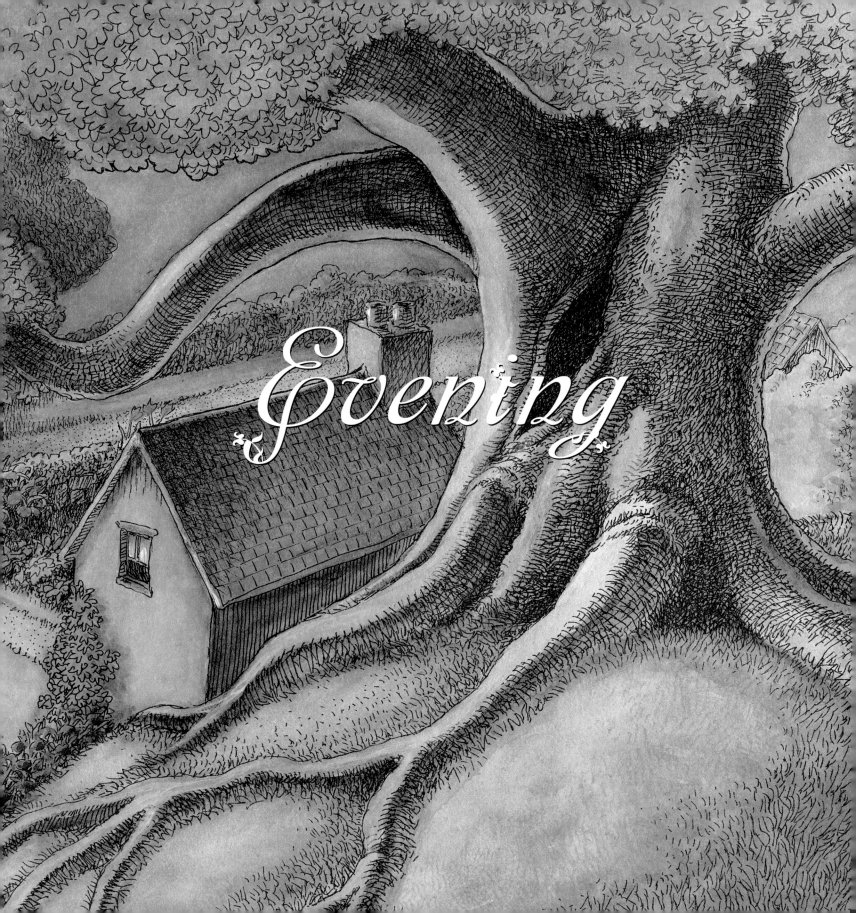

Budgie pulled weeds in the garden. Boo picked
vegetables for supper.

After they ate a delicious stew, Budgie and Boo decided to go for a walk. Night had come, and a full moon rose into the sky.

"The moon is so bright," Boo said.
"I won't even need my flashlight," said Budgie.

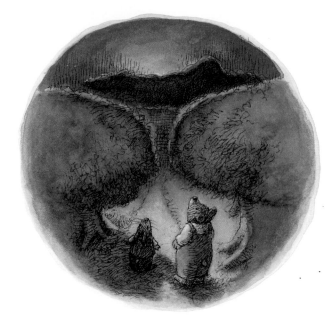

As they walked, suddenly their path became very dark.
"Boo, I'm scared," said Budgie. "I can't even see you."
"I'm scared, too," said Boo. "Shall we run?"
"It's too dark to run," answered Budgie. "We might trip and fall."

Just then a raindrop fell from the sky.
"Now *my* nose is wet!" Budgie cried.
Boo looked up and saw that a rain
cloud had moved in front of the moon.

"Let's go back to our house," Boo suggested. "It doesn't
rain inside our house anymore."
"That's why you are my best friend," Budgie said.
"Why?" asked Boo.
"Because you always know how to fix things," said Budgie.

The cloud moved on, and the moon shone brightly once more.

"Were you really scared, Budgie?" asked Boo.
"Not really," Budgie said. "Were you?"
"Oh, no. Not at all," Boo answered.

Budgie and Boo laughed and walked home together.
"I think we will always be best friends," said Budgie.
"Me, too," said Boo. "Always."
And they were.